KU-470-566

First published 1991 as *Wheels* by Walker Books Ltd
87 Vauxhall Walk, London SE11 5HJ

This edition published 2016

1 3 5 7 9 10 8 6 4 2

© 1991 Shirley Hughes

The right of Shirley Hughes to be identified as
author/illustrator of this work has been asserted by her in
accordance with the Copyright, Designs and Patents Act 1988

This book has been typeset in Plantin

Printed and bound in Germany by GGP

All rights reserved. No part of this book may be reproduced,
transmitted or stored in an information retrieval system in
any form or by any means, graphic, electronic or mechanical,
including photocopying, taping and recording, without prior
written permission from the publisher.

British Library Cataloguing in Publication Data:
a catalogue record for this book is available from
the British Library

ISBN 978-1-4063-7464-3

www.walker.co.uk

NEW WHEELS FOR CARLOS

A Tale of Trotter Street

Shirley Hughes

WALKER BOOKS
AND SUBSIDIARIES

LONDON · BOSTON · SYDNEY · AUCKLAND

Spring at last! The Easter holidays had arrived and the wheels were out on Trotter Street. Sanjit Lal zipped along on his roller-skates, wearing a smart crash-helmet. Little Pete Patterson rode

his red tricycle, ring-a-ding-dinging
the bell to let everyone know he was
coming.

Harvey and Barney took turns on
Barney's skate-board and Mae pushed

her baby sister Holly in a brand new buggy.

Some of the big girls and boys had

wonderful, new full-size bikes, even racers!

They gathered at the corner to show them off. Carlos and Billy had their old bikes.

Billy's mum looked after Carlos in the school holidays, while *his* mum was at work. When she took Billy's baby brother to the park in the afternoon, Carlos and Billy came too and brought their bikes. They were not old enough to ride on the road, of course. It was too dangerous.

The park was the best place to ride. There was a smooth, wide path which went round the play area then into a steep slope. You could whizz down it, cornering at high speed, and free-wheel the rest of the way, past the old band-stand until, braking

gently, you ended up at the bottom by
the lake where the ducks swam.

The little kids playing and the mums
chatting on the benches and the old
lady who came to feed the birds all
stopped what they were
doing and stared
as Carlos and
Billy flew past.

Whooosh!

There was
a narrow,
humpbacked
bridge over the
lake. Carlos and

Billy thought it was exciting to race their bikes up one side and down the other. Sometimes Carlos won and sometimes Billy. But if Mr Low, the park-keeper, saw them, he soon put a stop to it.

He was very strict about people behaving well in his park. Mr Low did not seem to like fast riding at all, not even on the paths.

Orville, his assistant, was not quite so strict. Sometimes, when Mr Low went off to have a cup of tea in his hut, Orville would call out encouraging things to Carlos and Billy as they raced by.

All the same, Carlos and Billy both wished they had better bikes.

"You can get up a lot more speed on a big bike," said Billy. "They have gears too."

"I've seen one I like in a shop," said Carlos. "Blue and silver with a pump to match."

"I'm going to ask for a new bike for my birthday," said Billy. "It's very soon now."

"It's my birthday soon as well," said

Carlos, "and I'm going to get a new bike too."

Carlos asked his mum about this. He had asked her before and he asked her again that evening. But his mum said that new bikes were very expensive. She explained that it was difficult for her to save up for things like bikes. She worked in a bakery and often brought

home nice fruit cake and cream buns
for Carlos and his big brother Marco –
but not very much money.

"Marco's got a proper bike," moaned
Carlos.

"He's older than you," said Mum,
"and he needs it for his Saturday job.
He's saving up for a new mountain-bike.
When you're bigger, you can learn to
ride his old one."

"But I need a new bike *now*," Carlos
said.

Mum only answered: "We'll have
to see…"

On the afternoon of his birthday,
Billy proudly brought his brand new bike
to the park. It was orange, with shiny
silver handlebars. Everyone gathered
round to admire it. Even Orville left his
work to come and have a look at it.

"Race you!" Billy called out to Carlos, as he pulled away and glided off down the path.

It was not much of a race. Billy won easily. Carlos felt silly pedalling furiously behind, crouched over the handlebars of his old bike. His legs felt too long and his knees kept getting in the way.

After a while Billy's mum suggested that Billy should give Carlos a turn on his new bike, which he very kindly did.

But when Carlos had swooped down
the hill like a bird once or twice, he
had to give the beautiful bike back
to Billy.

In the end, Carlos gave up wanting
to race. There was no point. He threw
down his old bike by the lake and sat by
himself, tossing pebbles into the water.

He felt cross with Billy. He even felt cross with the ducks who came swimming over to see if he had any bread.

"You wait! You wait till it's my birthday!" he told them.

On the evening before his birthday, Carlos kept wondering if Mum had managed to get him a bike. He thought she could have hidden one in the shed behind their block of flats.

He even secretly slipped out and tried the shed door, but it was locked.

Was there a bike inside? He looked through a crack, but he couldn't see anything. Mum had promised that tomorrow she would bring home a very special cake from the shop – a birthday cake for Carlos! She said

that he could ask Billy round for tea.

But Carlos didn't want Billy to come

to his birthday tea.

In bed that night, Carlos was too excited to sleep.

He kept imagining getting a new bike: a big bike, a blue and silver bike, a bike that was even better and faster than Billy's, which he could show off in the park. He crept to the window and looked down at the shed. There was a light on in there! He could see it shining up through the skylight in the roof. He watched for a long time.

Then he went back to bed.

In the morning, Mum gave Carlos a big birthday hug. Marco had gone off early, but he had left a card on the kitchen table with some bears in a spaceship and "Happy Birthday, Carlos" written inside it. There were some parcels on the table too, all wrapped in fancy paper.

"Aren't you going to open them?" asked Mum, beaming.

Carlos pulled off the papers one by one. There was a jigsaw puzzle, a new jacket in dazzling red and green, just like the ones the big boy bikers wore,

and a toy car with remote control.
Carlos had wanted one ever since he
had seen them in a shop and he was
very pleased. But he knew at once that
there was no new bike.

"Marco's going to give you his

present when he comes in at teatime,"
Mum told him.

Carlos knew that Marco's present
could not possibly be a new bike.

He would not have nearly enough money for that. Inside, Carlos could not help feeling bitterly disappointed.

When Mum asked him if he would like to go and play with Billy that

morning and show him his new things,
Carlos said no – he would rather go
to the shop with Mum. So he took his
new car and played with it in the back
of the bakery while his mum served

the customers. The car went very well. Everyone made a great fuss of Carlos when they heard it was his birthday. One lady bought him a chocolate cream cake and another gave him some money for his piggy-bank.

When they got home, Mum opened a box and brought out a truly wonderful cake. It was pink and white and covered in icing shells and swirls, with

silver holders for the candles. There
was a plate of fancy pastries too,
and ice-cream. Carlos ate a lot of

everything. But when the time came to light his candles, he missed having Billy to help him blow them out.

Then Marco walked in. He got hold of Carlos and swung him round, singing "Happy Birthday to you!" Then he ate a very large slice of cake.

"Want to find out what I've got for you?" said Marco. "Follow me."

Carlos followed Marco downstairs.

All the way down, Carlos
was wondering what Marco
was going to give him.

He knew it could not be
a bike. So what was it? They
walked right past the shed.
Then at last Carlos saw
his present!

It was a go-cart! A real go-cart! It had proper steering and rubber wheels and a seat, and it was painted bright red. Marco had made it himself. Carlos was too surprised to speak. Never, ever, in his wildest dreams had he imagined owning a go-cart! He looked at it for a long time. He stroked its wheels and its little seat. Then he put his head against Marco's arm. "Thanks, Marco," he said.

It was the last day of the holidays. Most of Trotter Street had turned up in the park for the big event: the Non-Bicycle Race! The starters were

already lined up – Sanjit, Sam and
Ruby Roberts were on roller-skates;
Harvey and Barney had skate-boards.
Jim Zolinski and Brains Barrington

were in their box-on-wheels; Frankie
had borrowed a scooter, and Mae and
Debbie had one roller-skate each.
Carlos was at the controls of his new
go-cart, with Billy crouching behind him.
Now Josie lifted the starter's flag…

Ready, steady, GO!

Cheering mums,

dads and toddlers lined

the track. The Bird Lady was

there and Orville too. Even Mr Low

popped his head round the door of

his hut to watch, though mostly to

keep an eye on his flower-beds.

Past the play area, into the steep

slope, gaining speed then cornering

wildly, sometimes crashing but

managing to scramble on again,

weaving, coasting, trundling they

went – all the way down to the lake.

And who came first?

Carlos and Billy in the

wonderful go-cart,

of course!

Shirley Hughes has illustrated more than 200 children's books and is one of the world's best-loved writers for children. She has won the Kate Greenaway Medal twice and has been awarded an OBE for her distinguished service to children's literature. In 2007, *Dogger* was voted the UK's favourite Kate Greenaway Medal-winning book of all time.

"No one can match Shirley Hughes in the simple mastery of both words and pictures."
Times Educational Supplement